The Sleepover Club

Have you been invited to all these sleepovers?

Sleepover Girls Go Pop!

by Lorna Read

An imprint of HarperCollinsPublishers

The Sleepover Club ® is a registered trademark
of HarperCollins*Publishers* Ltd

First published as *The Sleepover Girls Go Spice*
in Great Britain by Collins in 1997
Collins is an imprint of HarperCollins*Publishers* Ltd,
77-85 Fulham Palace Road, Hammersmith,
London W6 8JB

The HarperCollins website address is
www.**fire**and**water**.com

1 3 5 7 9 8 6 4 2

Text copyright © Lorna Read 1997

Original series characters, plotlines
and settings © Rose Impey 1997

ISBN 0 00712621-2

Printed and bound in Great Britain by
Omnia Books Limited, Glasgow

Sleepover Kit List

1. Sleeping bag
2. Pillow
3. Pyjamas or a nightdress
4. Slippers
5. Toothbrush, toothpaste, soap etc
6. Towel
7. Teddy
8. A creepy story
9. Food for a midnight feast:
   chocolate, crisps, sweets, biscuits.
   In fact anything you like to eat.
10. Torch
11. Hairbrush
12. Hair things like a bobble or hairband,
    if you need them
13. Clean knickers and socks
14. Change of clothes for the next day
15. Sleepover diary and membership card

CHAPTER ONE

Uh-oh, I can see Frankie looking at me. Well, looking's hardly the word. She's glaring like Fliss's neighbour, Mr Watson-Wade - Mr Grumpy, as we call him - does, when he thinks we've thrown crisp packets into his pond.

I know what that look means. It means I've got to tell you the truth, the whole truth and nothing but the truth, cross my heart a billion, trillion, zillion times and hope to die before Andy - that's Fliss's mum's boyfriend - discovers that his guitar is really a cardboard cut-out and my brother Stuart discovers why his saxophone won't make a sound any more!

I'm a Libran and everybody knows Librans don't like telling lies. We're the ones who believe everybody should play fair. We're always trying to keep the peace - but 'peace' is a dirty word in our house at the moment. At least, since Saturday night.

It wasn't all our fault. It was partly Dad's, for not converting the attic properly.

He's always doing weird things to our house, like moving the doors around and building extra rooms. I shouldn't be surprised to wake up one day and find out he's double-glazed me!

I'm Lyndz, by the way. That's short for Lyndsey Marianne Collins. I'm one of the five members of the Sleepover Club.

The others are Laura McKenzie, known as Kenny. She's Frankie's best friend. There's Francesca Thomas, Frankie for short, and Fliss. Fliss's full name is Felicity Sidebotham (please don't laugh, it's not fair. Anyway, she pronounces it Side-both-am).

The last person to join our gang was Rosie, alias Rosie Maria Cartwright. It was my idea that she should be allowed to join, because she was new to the area, and new to school, and didn't know anyone.

Well, we had to rescue her from the dreaded M&Ms, didn't we? Just imagine if she'd got into the clutches of our worst enemies! The Goblin - that's Emily

Berryman, one of the M&Ms - might have twitched her stupid splodgy nose and turned her into a toad or something.

Quick! I've just noticed Frankie isn't looking. Let's run out into the garden and hide in the shed, otherwise she'll want to tell you everything as usual, and I won't get a turn.

Mum calls our shed the summerhouse, now that Dad's fixed a completely gross verandah on the front, with a wonky railing. Mum's put some old chairs in and painted them streaky blue. Mediterranean blue, she calls it. It looks more like what happened in Rosie's living room when it was being painted and Jenny, her dog, wagged her tail all over the wet wall.

Right. Now listen up, as my Canadian cousin Ryan would say. He sent us a tape with his voice on at Christmas and "listen up" was his fave expression. "Hey, listen up, the snow's fifteen feet deep outside our door." Well, if the snow was that thick all round the house, the only sound you'd hear would be from up above, anyway. You'd be walking round lop-sided, with one ear raised to the ceiling, listening up for the rescue helicopters!

But it's me who needs rescuing right

11

now, so stop slurping that Slush-Puppy and popping that bubble-gum and I'll tell you what you really want to know.

Oh no, I've done it now! Tell me what you want, what you really, really want... That's a bit of Wannabe, by the Spice Girls. And that, unfortunately, is where the whole thing began.

Oops! I've got hiccups now and when I hic, I really, really hic. It's your fault. You shouldn't have made me laugh. What you've got to do for me now is press your thumbs very hard into the palm of my hand while I hold my breath.

There, it's worked. Not a hic in sight (or sound). As I was saying, we - the Sleepovers, that is - are crazy about the Spice Girls at the moment. In a few weeks or months, we might be crazy about somebody else, but right now, Spice is nice as far we we're concerned.

Sometimes we sneak into the studio at school when it's empty at dinnertime. We love to dance, and sometimes Dishy Dave the caretaker plays the piano for us. He's really good. He plays all these pop songs by ear. Well, with his fingers, actually. Oh no, don't make me hiccup again! We asked him if he knew any Spice Girls songs and he did. He said he really likes them, too, and he'd got their video.

He asked us what our favourite Spice song was and we had a big argument. Fliss and I love Mama. Kenny's fave is Wannabe and Rosie and Frankie think Love Thing is brilliant. Dave decided Mama was the easiest for him to play, because it's slow.

The studio's got mirrors on the walls so that dancers and gymnasts can watch themselves performing. We all struck Spice Girl poses and sang the words. Kenny can sing quite loud, though she often goes flat. Fliss and Rosie have got soft, whispery voices, but at least they're in tune.

Frankie sounds like a crow with laryngitis. No wonder she wrote in her Sleepover diary a while back that she'd given up wanting to be a pop star when she grew up and wanted to drive a taxi instead!

As for me, I think I'm a good singer. Yes, I know I sound as if I'm boasting, but I was given a solo to sing in the Nativity show last Christmas and Mrs Weaver would never have given it to me if she thought I sounded like Mary and Joseph's donkey. (Frankie does.)

Dave thought we were good. "That's great! You sound just like them," he said.

"There's five of you, too, just like the five Spice Girls. You should start a group," he said.

So, really, if we're blaming anybody, we should blame Dishy Dave for getting the ball rolling, the cookie crumbling, the group grouping ...

Okay, okay. I know I'm rambling. Please don't fall asleep, though. I haven't got a Sleepover planned for tonight. In fact, after last Friday, I don't think my parents are going to allow one here ever again!!!

CHAPTER TWO

Right from the start, it was intended to be our thing. 'Girl Power', as the Spice Girls would say. The last thing we wanted was to get mixed up with a gang of horrible, smelly boys, even if some of them were my own brothers.

You should get a whiff of Tom's room. He's my second oldest brother, aged 14. Old socks and stale crisps. Steve, who's sixteen and my oldest brother, smells of zit cream and stinky feet, because he hates having baths.

I once made a sign for Tom's door. It had a skull and crossbones on it and under it I wrote, NASAL DEATH AREA. He took it down and ripped it up, leaving all the family noses in mortal danger once more.

Fliss and Rosie have got brothers, too, so

a few weeks ago I decided to try and find out if all brothers smell, or if it's just my personal misfortune. Fliss said that Callum, her seven-year-old brother, smells like stink bombs. My little brother Ben smells of wee, and as for baby Spike - well, he often smells of worse, when his nappy needs changing!

Rosie's got the perfect brother. Although Adam's got cerebral palsy and is in a wheelchair, he's fanatical about his appearance. He loves taking showers and having his hair moussed and gelled and the best prezzie you can give him is a really nice spray cologne. I wish my brothers would catch the habit!

It's not as if nobody ever gives Tom and Stuart any smellies. They're always getting them for Christmas and birthdays, but the minute they put them on, the scent mutates into Dead Rat or something.

Not that they often use their smellies on themselves. They do stupid things with them instead, like the time Stuart decided our cats' litter tray ponged and wasted a whole bottle of Dad's Aramis, trying to freshen it up.

Unfortunately, right in the middle of his spraying activities, Toffee came bounding through the cat flap and caught a full blast.

Fudge and Truffle, our other two cats, treated him like an alien and wouldn't go near him for days, and Buster, our dog, got a sneezing attack whenever Toffee sat next to him.

Anyway, back to that afternoon three weeks ago, which is when it all began...

The bell for the end of dinnertime had rung and we all said a reluctant goodbye to our reflections in the mirror and started to walk back to our classroom.

Fliss was the last one to leave the studio, of course. She just had to pout at herself and toss her ponytail one last time. She gave a high kick through the studio door and lost her balance and nearly fell over. As she tottered around with her arms whirling like windmills, who should stroll past but the lurv of her life, Ryan Scott.

"Hi there, Fliss. They'll never have you in the Riverdance team," he said, sniggering.

You should have seen her blush. It was just as if someone had thrown tomato ketchup in her face! Frankie gave me a big nudge and I nearly fell over, too.

"Drunk again, Lyndsey," said Ryan.

"Oh, run off and play on the M1, won't you?" said Frankie, in her best "you're being really bo-ring" voice.

He shrugged and did a big slide round the corner of the corridor, with his hands in his pockets. I was hoping Mrs Lynch would be coming round the corner and he'd go wham, straight into her, but no such luck.

Mrs Lynch is our school secretary and she's seriously bad-tempered, not like Mrs Poole, our Head. She's a sweetie, unless you do something really bad, and then she can get you expelled!

"Why did you have to be nasty to him? He'll think we don't like him now!" Fliss complained.

"I think you're a very sad person, Fliss," Frankie told her, and a row was all set to break out, until Kenny changed the subject. Thank goodness she did. Who wants to talk about boring boys? Especially big-headed posers like Ryan Scott!

What Kenny said was all set to change our lives, though none of us knew it at the time.

"Do you think Dave meant it?" she asked us.

Rosie frowned. "Meant what?"

"About us being like the Spice Girls."

"I hope so!" said Fliss.

"Stoo-pid!" said Frankie.

"Why does it matter?" I asked Kenny.

"The competition!" Kenny said.

We all stared at her. Then I suddenly remembered. I don't watch much telly. I'm not as mad about it as the rest of the club, especially Fliss, who eats, drinks and sleeps Friends and has all the episodes on video - she's the saddest thing on earth! One thing I do enjoy, though, is seeing people make complete twits of themselves on Stars in Their Eyes, where they have to look and sound like a famous singer.

The other day Mrs Poole announced in Assembly that the school was going to raise some money to send some needy kids in a children's home on holiday.

"The staff and I have had a discussion and we've come up with something we thought you'd all enjoy," she told us. "Every class is going to enter an act in Cuddington Primary's version of Stars in Their Eyes. There'll be class heats first and we want all of you to have a go. The winning act from every class will get a prize, and they'll perform in the charity show. The ticket money will go to the children's home."

We didn't think any more about it, as none of us are particularly talented, though Fliss thinks she looks and sings like Madonna and Frankie plays pretty mean piano.

But it looked as if Frankie had thought of something now, and the rest of us were desperate to find out what it was.

The door of our classroom was closing as we got to it. I grabbed the handle to stop the others from entering, while I thought quickly.

"Six o'clock at my place, folks," I told everyone. "Mum's got yoga tonight and Dad'll be in the workshop. He's trying to finish this really gross pot for Auntie Cath's birthday. I don't know what she'll ever use it for."

My dad really fancies himself as an arty potter, but his efforts are always wobbly and lopsided, or bits drop off them. They are totally useless, though he thinks they're works of art which should be worth millions of pounds and displayed in museums throughout the world.

"A spaghetti jar?" suggested practical Fliss.

"A potty?" Rosie giggled.

"That's what your dad is – a potty potter," Frankie said.

We all laughed loudly, even me, though it was my dad Frankie was insulting.

Then Mrs Weaver yelled, "When you girls feel like joining us, the class can start."

So we had to go in and pretend to be interested in caddis fly larvae.

As we were drawing them in our Nature Study books, Frankie made hers look like my baby brother Spike, swaddled in an enormous nappy. I tried so hard not to laugh when she passed it to me under the desk that I got the hiccups.

Mrs Weaver sent Alana Banana, of all people, to get me a glass of water, but my hand shook so much as I hiccuped, that the water shot all over the back of Emma Hughes, one of the M&Ms.

That put the king in the cake all right! She's one of our worst enemies and the sight of water dripping down her neck inside her collar made us have hysterics. We just collapsed with our heads on our desks and sobbed.

But it stopped my hiccups, so it was a good thing for me, if not for Emma, who hissed, "I'll get you for this, Lyndsey Collins! You've really got it coming!"

Now, a threat from the M&Ms spells real doom. I had no doubt in my mind that Emma and her crony Emily meant to do something to get back at me.

But what...?

CHAPTER THREE

I laid the news on Mum as soon as I got home.

"No way. You can't have all your friends round tonight," she said.

"But why not?" I wailed. "I've invited them now. It's not fair!"

"I've got some of my friends coming this evening. I might be an old wrinkly, but I do have friends, you know, and I'm going to be far too busy entertaining them to cater for you lot as well," she insisted.

"I thought it was your yoga night and we wouldn't be in the way," I said.

"It's been cancelled. The teacher's on holiday."

I put on my sweetest, most pleading face. "Please, Mum... They'll have eaten already by the time they get here. And we won't take up any space. We'll go straight up to my room and disappear. We're having a summit conference," I told her importantly.

"The summit of stupidity, if you ask me!" snorted Tom, who would happen to walk into the kitchen right then.

"It is not!" I said angrily.

"'Tis."

"'Tisn't!"

"Oh, stop being babyish, you two," said Mum. "Look, if you want to see your friends tonight, Lyndsey, just make sure they bring their own crisps and biscuits, and keep out of the lounge at all costs. Okay?"

"Thanks, Mum!" I said, giving her a hug.

Frankie's dad brought her, Kenny and Rosie over. Shortly afterwards, Andy, Fliss's mum's boyfriend, dropped Fliss off.

I'd already done a phone around about the food situation, and raided some of the emergency rations Mum keeps in the spare fridge, which sits next to the huge freezer in the garage.

I'd found a big tub of my favourite ice-cream, two packets of chocolate biscuits and a bumper crisp selection pack. Don't ask me why there were crisps in the fridge. I guess Mum was being hassled by Ben and

Spike and just shoved them anywhere to get rid of them. The crisps, I mean, not my little brothers.

Frankie's dad brought in a six-pack of Cokes. Fliss had some bananas and a bottle of diet lemonade so I knew she had to be on one of her healthy eating kicks again. Rosie had some Jaffa Cakes. Kenny was carrying a weird looking cake. It was sort of pinky orange.

"Ugh! What's that?" I asked her.

"Molly made it at school. It's supposed to be carrot cake," she explained. Molly is Kenny's twelve-year-old sister.

"It's bound to be horrible," Fliss said. "She wouldn't have let you have it if it hadn't been. You know how much she hates us. She's probably trying to poison us so she'll never have to move out of the bedroom again."

Molly and Kenny share a room and every time we spend the night there, she has to move in with Emma, Kenny's oldest sister. Both of them hate having to share, and Molly's always nasty about which of her possessions we mustn't touch or go anywhere near. Last time we had a sleepover at Kenny's, Molly was so strict about her precious Spanish costume doll that,

24

after she'd gone, I took its knickers off and made it a little nappy out of some pieces of toilet paper held together with a safety pin.

She can't have discovered it yet, otherwise she'd have gone ballistic and I'd have heard all about it from Kenny.

I made everyone take off their shoes before going in my room. We always kick our shoes off, anyway, and my room's too small for loads of shoes. There's no space to put anything and Dad still hasn't made me the new bedroom in the attic he's been promising me for over a year.

I took the cake off Kenny and looked for somewhere to put it, where it wouldn't get damaged. My dressing table was far too full of stuff, so in the end I put the cake down on the floor, between the bottom of the bed and the window. Big mistake.

Meanwhile, everyone was cramming themselves on to my bed and on the carpet. There was no room for Rosie till we'd closed the door and she could sit with her back to it. That was great, because it meant no nosy brothers could get in.

Frankie remained standing. It was obvious she wanted to organise everything as usual.

"I've got this great idea," she announced.

We all groaned. This was one of Frankie's stock phrases, and it always led to trouble of some sort.

She ignored us. "How many Spice Girls are there?" she asked.

"Five, of course," said Rosie.

"How many of us are there?"

"Five," said Kenny, frowning.

Frankie grinned. Then she ripped open a crisp packet noisily and started cramming the contents into her mouth.

I sighed. Frankie loved 'keeping us in suspenders', as she put it.

"Come on," I said. "Give us a clue."

"Mm-mm-mm-mm," she muttered through her munching.

"What?" we asked her.

She gave a big gulp and licked her crumby lips.

"Stars in Their Eyes," she replied. "School version, of course. Why don't we go in for it as the Spice Girls?"

"Yeah! Fantastic! Can I be Baby Spice?" yelled Fliss.

She took a flying leap off the end of the bed. There was a squelchy sound. Then silence. Then an awful scream. She'd landed right in Molly's carrot cake and squashed it all over the carpet. Fliss is very fussy, just like her mother. She absolutely hates getting in a mess. When we saw bits of creamy orange sponge squidging between her bare toes, we all collapsed.

"Oh no, oh no, I think I'm going to wet myself," giggled Rosie, which made us all laugh even more.

Then I heard Mum coming up the stairs.

"Girls, girls, what's going on up here? Is everything all right?" she called out.

"Yes, yes," I panted, between hoots of laughter. "Fliss just put her foot in it, that's all!"

Luckily for us, the doorbell rang. Mum dashed down the stairs to answer it, giving me a chance to get a sponge from the bathroom and do some cleaning up.

When we'd all calmed down, we got down to some serious snacking and talking.

"Who's going to be who, then?" asked Kenny.

"I think you should be Sporty Spice," Frankie told her.

Although we all like sports and all play netball, Kenny is seriously sports mad. She never wears anything but jeans and sportswear. Tonight, she was wearing jeans and a Leicester City Football Club sweatshirt. They're her favourite team. My dad and grandad are mad about them, too, and sometimes we all go to matches together.

We all agreed that Kenny was perfect for Sporty Spice and, to save arguments, we agreed that Fliss could be Baby Spice. She has the right colour of hair, after all.

It was a bit difficult choosing Ginger Spice, because none of us has got ginger hair. But my mum has a big trunk full of dressing up clothes, amongst which is a red wig she bought to wear at a fancy dress party. I felt sure she'd let me borrow it. So I became Ginger Spice.

We all thought Frankie was perfect for Scary Spice, because she's such an extrovert. Although she doesn't wear glasses, she's got some sunglasses that the lenses keep falling out of. So she said she could just wear the frames.

"Don't think I'm going to get my tongue pierced, though," she said, with a shudder.

"You could stick a blob of chewing gum on it, to look as if it was," suggested Kenny.

"Yes but when I sang, it would go flying out into the audience," Frankie said.

"It might hit one of the M&Ms," said Rosie, giggling at the thought.

"Right in the eye, with any luck," I said.

Frankie laughed and spluttered crisps everywhere. As usual, we were all getting covered in crumbs. It's as if, when we get into a room together, we become grot magnets and pick up every crumb, foodstain and drip going. It's like magic. I think every bit of dropped food and spilt drink in the universe looks around and says, "Oh look, it's the Sleepover Club, let's go get 'em!" and they all come whirling in our direction and go splot, all over us.

Four Spice Girls were decided. That left Rosie to be Posh Spice.

"But I'm not posh!" she protested.

"Your hair's the right colour, though," Fliss pointed out.

"Okay. Now, how about our clothes?" Frankie said. She was being the boss, as usual. None of us really minded, though. At least she got things done, so the rest of us could be lazy.

"Kenny's all right, she can just wear what she normally wears," said Fliss.

"And so can you, Fliss," Rosie said. "That silver dress of yours is a bit like one that Emma wears."

By 'Emma', she meant Baby Spice, of course, not Emma of the dreaded M&Ms, my very worst and dreadest enemy!

"There's always Mum's dressing-up box," I said. "Anything we haven't got, we're bound to find in there. She's even got some genuine stripy T-shirts from last time they were in fashion."

"Cool," said Frankie.

"Now that we've decided who we all are, how are we going to do our show? Mime to one of their records?" I asked.

"No way. I want to sing!" insisted Fliss.

The rest of us glared at her. We didn't want to sing and get laughed at by all the boys in our school. Of course, she hoped Ryan Scott would hear her wonderful voice and fall madly in love with her. I tell you, Fliss is saddest of the sad!

"We've got to sing. They do on Stars in Their Eyes," said Rosie. "Besides, I want to sing Say You'll Be There."

"No, we've got to do Wannabe!" yelled Frankie.

"Mama," begged Fliss.

"Okay, okay," Kenny said. "Tell you what we'll do. We'll put the CD on and try them all out and see which one we do the best."

We soon found we had a mega problem. The louder we sang, the louder we had to turn the volume up in order to hear the Spice Girls. And the more we turned it up, the louder we had to sing, until we were screeching at the tops of our voices.

I switched the machine off in the middle of Mama.

"It's no good," I said. "We'll just have to mime."

"No, no!" Fliss wailed.

"Or else get hold of a karaoke tape with just the music on," suggested Frankie.

That was the best idea anyone had had all day. In fact, we were so happy about it that we decided to eat our tub of ice cream, which was busy melting.

Before we could even pick up a spoon, doom struck in the shape of my oldest brother, Stuart. He hammered on my door and yelled, "Hey, Lyndz, you haven't seen the food that was in the fridge in the garage, have you?"

My hand shot to my mouth and I felt quite ill.

Fliss let out a squeak like an electrocuted mouse.

Frankie groaned, "Oh, no," then we all tried to be as quiet as anything.

But it was no good. Stu came barging in, totally ignoring my Keep Out notice on the door.

"Aha! Thought as much!" he said,

swooping on the ice cream. Luckily, we hadn't even got the lid off yet.

"I'll have those chocolate biscuits, please. And the big bag of crisps," he demanded.

"Er..." I went. The others had gone bright pink and were starting to giggle. "Shut up!" I hissed at them.

I saw Kenny trying to push the remains of one of the biscuit packets under the bed, but I had so much junk over there that it wouldn't go.

"Don't tell me you've scoffed the lot?" Stu said. "I've got Tony and Mick here for band practice. That food was for us. I bought it and hid it specially so that greedy pigs like you and Tom wouldn't find it."

I looked at my feet, wishing they'd disappear through a hole in the ground, with me following them. But no such luck.

"Sorry," I said. "How was I expected to know that stuff was yours? Put your name on it next time."

"Two pound fifty, that lot cost me. You can jolly well pay me back!" he said.

He went out, going, "Piglets. Oink, oink."

I could hear his foul friends laughing. Foul fiends, I should say. Who'd have brothers?

CHAPTER FOUR

Next day, Mrs Weaver, our class teacher, said that anyone who intended to enter an act for the charity show had to tell her by the following day.

Frankie put her hand up. "Can we tell you now, Mrs Weaver?" she asked.

"Of course, Frankie," Mrs Weaver replied.

I looked round. I could see everyone was bursting with curiosity. Especially the M&Ms. Emma's eyes were just about popping out of her head and Emily's ears were flapping like Dumbo the elephant's.

"We don't want everyone to know, though. We want to keep it a secret," I said.

Mrs Weaver smiled and said, "I see. Then write down what you want to do and give it to me."

Frankie tore a page out of her general

33

notebook and started scribbling. She folded it up and passed it to Mrs Weaver, who unfolded it and started to read it.

My heart was racing. Please don't give the game away, PLEASE! I begged her silently, trying to use telepathic powers to get through to her.

Well, they'll never write an X-Files story about me, because my extra-sensory powers are obviously nil. The next moment, Mrs Weaver put her foot right in it by saying to Frankie, "So there's you, Felicity, Laura, Lyndsey and who's the fifth girl? I can't read your writing."

The five of us looked at each other in panic.

"It's me," Rosie squeaked.

"Rosie Cartwright," said Mrs Weaver, writing it down.

I saw the M&Ms exchange excited glances. Emma gave Emily a big smirk.

Emily - The Goblin, as we call her - nudged The Queen (that's Emily), who in turn nudged Banana, alias Alana Palmer. Then she said nastily, "I hope you don't think you're going to be the Spice Girls. We're going to be the Spice Girls. That was our idea. They pinched it, Mrs Weaver."

Kenny gave a gasp and jumped to her

feet. "We never did!" she said. "Don't tell porkies!"

I jumped up, too. "We decided days ago. We've already been practising!" I said.

Mrs Weaver waved her hand. "Now, now, girls, stop arguing," she said. "There can be more than one Spice Girls act, and may the best one win!"

Emma, my personal worst enemy since yesterday when I'd spilt water down her stupid neck, turned round. She screwed up her face and her horrid, blobby nose so that she looked like a squashed tomato, poked out her tongue at me and said, "See?"

I pulled a face back.

"So I take it you and your friends want to be the Spice Girls, too?" Mrs Weaver said.

"Yes please, Mrs Weaver," replied The Goblin, in her most sucking-up tones. Creep! She's just pathetic.

"And who else will be singing with you?" asked Mrs Weaver.

The M&Ms nudged their slave, the slimy Banana, and she put her hand up.

I looked at Rosie. She was giggling. "They've only got three Spice Girls," she said.

"I'll join you, if you like."

We all stared as Regina Hill spoke. Even

the M&Ms stared. Regina hasn't been in our class for long. Her family have only just moved to Cuddington from London and we don't know much about her, especially as she's rather quiet. So everyone was amazed when she spoke.

"Can you sing?" Emma asked her.

You could have knocked me down with a King Cone when Regina began to sing Summer Nights from Grease, all perfectly in tune. She had an awesome voice.

My eyes met Frankie's. Then I looked at Fliss, Kenny and Rosie. Everyone had the same look on their faces. Hate, pure hate.

"It's not fair!" I said at break.

"We decided to be the Spice Girls first," Frankie said crossly.

"They're just pathetic copy-cats," said Rosie, flicking her brown fringe.

"Yes, they are," Fliss added.

"Reggie-Veggie's got a good voice, though," I said.

"Reggie-Veggie! That's a good name for her," said Frankie, with a loud snort that made us all laugh. "What kind of a vegetable do you think she is?"

"A carrot," Fliss said promptly.

"Well, she is long and thin - and her hair is kind of reddish," I agreed. Before today, we'd thought she was really pretty and she'd seemed quite nice, but she'd certainly turned into a carrot now that she'd become a friend of the M&Ms.

"You know what this means, don't you?" Frankie said gloomily.

We looked at her and shook our heads. We'd never felt so depressed.

"If they're going to sing, we can't get away with only miming. We'll jolly well have to sing, too."

"Oh, no!" Kenny wailed.

"Oh good," said Fliss. "I think I sing better than Reggie-Veggie!"

We knew she wanted us to pay her compliments, but we were all fed up so nobody did.

Fliss went into a sulk and got her Banana-In-Pyjamas toy out of her bag. Her aunt in America sent it to her. Bananas In Pyjamas are very popular in America, according to Fliss's aunt. Personally, I think dressed up plastic bananas are stupid. Give me a toy pony any day. Better still, a real one.

Fliss started creating a little wedding veil for the banana, out of a piece of paper tissue. She's mad on weddings. All her toys and stuffed animals have been married at least twenty times each, to different partners. It's about time she started giving them divorces, not weddings.

I decided to cheer her up. "Of course you sing well, Fliss. We all know that."

"Perhaps we ought to give up on being the Spice Girls and think of something else," said Rosie.

"What? Give up? No way!" said Frankie. "We're not going to let ourselves be beaten by the M&Ms, are we?"

Nobody answered.

Frankie sat down on the concrete of the playground. Her bottom just missed a piece of chewing gum. She pulled a notebook and pen out of her black nylon shoulderbag. We all sat round her as she wrote two headings on the page.

The first heading said, Us. The second said, The M&Ms.

"Right," she said. "Now, think of all the reasons why our Spice Girls group is better than theirs."

"We're better than them at everything!" I said.

"We can sing," said Fliss.

"We're the greatest," said Rosie.

38

"They're ugly," said Kenny, and we all fell about.

"Now tell me why they're worse than us," Kenny said.

"They're ugly," said Kenny again.

When we'd stopped laughing for the second time, I said, "And pathetic."

"And copy-cats, weeds and nerds," said Fliss.

"Is this war?" asked Frankie.

"This is WAR!" we all agreed.

That night I told my mum about it. Maybe I chose a wrong moment. At the time, she was battling with a curtain that had got stuck in one of the holes inside the washing machine.

"Mm, dear. Help me with this, could you?" was all she said.

I got my head inside the machine. A corner of the material was jammed. I had a hair grip in my pocket, from my last trip to the swimming baths. I always used grips to pin my hair under my swimming cap.

I poked the grip down the hole to loosen the bunched-up material, and promptly lost it.

"Oh, that's just wonderful!" said Mum sarkily. "That's going to rattle round in there forever, now. I'll hear it every time I use the machine."

"If I use one of the fridge magnets, I might be able to get it out," I said.

I thought it was a brilliant suggestion.

Mum didn't seem to agree. "Don't you go magnetising my washing machine, Lyndsey. It's all metal in there. Every zip will stick to the drum and I won't be able to get anyone's jeans out," she said.

I had a mental image of Mum and me, each hauling on a jeans' leg, trying to pull it out of the machine. I started laughing. Then my hiccups started.

"Oh, per-lease! Not those again," said Mum.

She rolled her eyes up to the ceiling and looked so weird that I laughed and hicked even harder.

"Sor-hic-ry," I apologised.

Mum was still tugging at the curtain. Suddenly, it came free and she fell over and landed on her bottom on the floor. I roared with laughter, it was so funny.

She gave me a hurt look. "How do you know I haven't broken anything?" she said.

"You haven't got any bones in your bottom," I pointed out.

I should have remembered that Mum

knows all about anatomy, as she teaches childbirth classes.

"I might have cracked my coccyx!" she said, which made me screech so much, I nearly had an accident. But it cured my hiccups, it really did.

I wandered out to the workshop to find Dad. I told him about what the M&Ms had done to us.

"You've just got to be better than them," he said, and started to sing Tina Turner's, Simply The Best. Now, Dad really can't sing, so I put my fingers in my ears. When I took them out again he was saying a very rude word because he'd dropped his paintbrush and the pot he was painting got a big green squiggle all down it.

"Never mind. Make it look like a piece of seaweed," I suggested.

"Seaweed? It was meant to be a leaping panther," he said grumpily

If that green blob was meant to be a panther, then I'm a Brussels sprout! Still, I said nothing. I didn't want to upset his artistic temperament. Besides, I needed to ask for extra pocket money, to make up for what I'd had to give Stu!

Then I remembered a really important question I had to ask.

"Dad," I said. "Do you know where I can get a karaoke tape of the Spice Girls' songs?"

"Haven't a clue," he said. He was being a real grump-pot. I knew his runny green panther had something to do with it.

So I rang Kenny. We'd all agreed to ask our parents about karaoke tapes and report back to her.

"You were my last hope, Lyndz," she said sadly. "Have you asked Stu?"

I wouldn't have thought of asking my rotten brother if the sky was blue, because I knew I'd never get the right answer. But everything was hanging on it. "I'll report back later. Roger. Over and out," I said.

Stu's so-called 'band' was driving everyone in our house crazy. I'd seen various band members arrive and when I went up to my room, I could hear them thumping about in the attic. There was a twang and a crash, as if the guitar fell over, then a sound as if someone had dropped the drums.

And just then, like the lottery finger coming down and saying, "It's you!", I got a fantastic, ginormous, amazing idea as to how the Sleepover Club could beat everyone, especially the M&Ms, and win the school competition...

CHAPTER FIVE

The only person I managed to get on the phone was Fliss. Everyone else was out.

"We've drawn a blank on the karaoke tapes but I've thought of something else," I told her.

"Tell me, tell me," she squeaked.

I didn't. Not straight away, anyway. Another brilliant bright idea had dawned.

"Lyndz? Are you still there?" I could hear Fliss saying.

"Yeah," I answered. Then I said, "I don't suppose by any teeny-weeny chance that you fancy the idea of a sleepover?"

"Do I? You bet! When?"

"Friday? Saturday? The sooner the better. We've got to start practising," I said.

"The class heats are in two weeks' time," she said gloomily.

Talk about dropping a bombshell! I was gobsmacked. Two weeks? We'd never have our act ready by then. Why had nobody told me?

I said those same words to Fliss.

"But Mrs Weaver mentioned it yesterday, just after all that trouble with the M&Ms," she said.

"I suppose I wasn't listening. My mind was full of hate. Kill, kill, kill! Death to the M&Ms!" I said dramatically.

"Was that what you rung me about, then? No, not about killing the M&Ms. The sleepover?" she asked me.

"No. I only just thought of that. My other great, earth-shattering idea was about the music to go with our song," I said.

"I know. You're going to ask the Spice Girls' band to play for us, I suppose," she said.

"Ho, ho. Don't be a moron," I told her. "I was listening to Stu and his friends playing the other night and - "

"You're not going to ask them?" she said. There was pure horror in her voice, as if I'd told her the M&Ms were about to be fried in toad juice and served up to her for lunch.

"Of course not! Can you imagine my big brother even setting foot in Cuddington

Primary? It would ruin his street cred for all time! But it made me think, why don't we accompany ourselves? We could borrow a guitar, and Frankie's got a keyboard..."

"But none of us can play the guitar," she pointed out.

"I know four chords. Stu showed me," I said proudly. "That's why the sleepover's got to be held here, so he can teach me some more. Will you tell Rosie and Kenny, and I'll keep trying to get Frankie. See you later, alligator!"

"In a while, crocodile," she replied.

"Have a laugh, big giraffe!" I said. It was our latest signing-off game. We kept trying to think of new animals.

"Don't get smelly pants, elephant!"

I snorted down the phone and laughed so loud, I must have deafened her. When I'd stopped laughing, which took ages, I told her I couldn't think of any more animals.

"Don't get fat, tabby cat. 'Bye!" she said, and rang off.

I stared at the receiver after she'd gone. Then I stared at the Twix bar in my other hand. How did she know I was about to eat it? It's not as if I've got a reputation for pigging out all the time... is it?

I searched the telephone for a tiny hidden

camera that could have relayed a piccy of my choc bar, but there wasn't one, of course. It was just my paranoia at being the fattest of us five friends.

Rosie's the next fattest, she's just sort of normal. Kenny is all muscle, Fliss is a natural stick insect, and Frankie is so tall that a few spare pounds wouldn't show. She's the luckiest, I think. I hope I grow taller soon.

My next big challenge was to ask Mum and Dad if I could have a sleepover. Although I kept my fingers crossed, I didn't need to because Mum was great about it.

"You know I love having the house full of girls, instead of horrid, smelly boys," she said.

I'm glad she agrees with me about boys. It must be because she's given birth to four of them - and got Dad and our dog to cope with, too!

She repeated another of her favourite sayings: "Girls are far less trouble than boys."

Though she didn't know it, she was going to regret saying that...

Next day was Saturday. We had all arranged to go to the library in the centre of

Cuddington at the same time, eleven o'clock in the morning.

I'm the furthest away, as I live in Little Wearing, whereas the others live in Cuddington itself. So I had to ask if someone would drive me over.

Dad volunteered, as he wanted to go to the art shop and buy some paints. He probably needed more green, after his accident with the leaping panther. Why paint a panther green, anyway? I suppose that's what you call 'artistic licence'.

When Dad dropped me off at the library, saying he'd pick me up in an hour, I could see two familiar bicycles fastened to the rail outside - Kenny's and Frankie's. Frankie has a new one. It's bright green, to go with her vegetarian nature. She eats so much salad that we kid her that she'll turn green one day. All over, including her hair, just like Dad's stupid panther.

We met in the music section, by the CD and tape selection.

"Look what I've found!" yelled Kenny, earning a warning frown from the man on the check-out desk.

It was a CD of football anthems. As you know, Kenny's seriously football mad. But this pointed to her being just plain mad, as well.

"Ugh! You're not actually thinking of listening to that, are you?" I said. "It'll do your eardrums in."

"I find football songs inspiring," she said mysteriously.

"Oh, get her!" said Rosie.

"Haven't they got a tape on teaching yourself to sing?" I said.

Frankie was looking very pleased with herself.

"I've gone one better than that," she said.

She waved two books at me. One was called, The Piano: Learn To Play in a Week. The other was called Guitar Made Easy.

"One for you and one for me," she said.

"I don't need that," I said, pointing to the guitar book. "You know I can play some chords."

"Yes, we've heard you," said Fliss.

She was referring to a time when we'd all been round at her place and Andy, had left his guitar lying around. He only ever got it out when Fliss's mum was out, as she hated hearing him play and thought guitars made the room look untidy.

I'd picked it up and played my four chords. I thought I sounded brilliant, but when I looked round, they all had their fingers jammed in their ears and were making being sick noises. Call themselves friends? I ask you!

"Let's get the books out, anyway," said Frankie. "I certainly need to improve a bit."

"Don't forget to bring your keyboard next Friday," I reminded her. It was only small, so it was easy to carry.

"Friday's nearly a week off. Couldn't we have a practice tomorrow?" Kenny said desperately.

Our parents would only ever let us have sleepovers at weekends, so there was no chance at all of us having a proper get-together before then, if Sunday was out.

It looked as if it was, worse luck.

"I can't," Rosie said. "We're going out for the day with my gran and grandad."

"And I'm going to Alton Towers for Carl and Colin's birthday," Fliss said, then waited for our reaction.

A chorus of "You lucky thing!" came from the rest of us.

Then I thought about Carl and Colin, Fliss's twin cousins. They were a gruesome twosome, the male equivalent of the M&Ms, as they were always poking fun at Fliss and being horrid to her. Maybe she wasn't so lucky, after all!

CHAPTER SIX

You're in school with me now. It's dinnertime. Come down the corridor with me. Ssh! Don't make any noise. Careful, your shoes are squeaking! We don't want anyone to hear.

Stop! We're right outside the door of the studio. Can you hear the the din that's going on in there? How could you miss it? It's like a load of groaning hippopotamuses - or should that be hippopotami? It's the M&Ms practising their Spice Girls routine. They're doing Wannabe and it's really pathetic.

Let's push the door open a crack and watch them dancing. They look like hippos, don't they, as well as sounding like them!

Just look at them galumphing about!

They've got old Fatty-Bum-Bum with them, which is what we call Amanda Porter. The nickname may sound a bit cruel, but you don't know Amanda. She's a horrible person, really nasty to everyone. We wouldn't care that she bought her dresses from Tents R us, if she was nice with it. But she hasn't got the niceness gene in her entire vast body. I don't know which Spice Girl she's meant to be. There isn't a Gross Spice, is there?

The only decent one among them is Regina Hill. She's not only got a good voice, she's obviously had some dancing lessons, too. Why did she have to offer to sing with them? They'd have been booed out of school if it hadn't been for her. I wish she could have sung with us. If only the Spice Girls would suddenly add a sixth girl to their group. Then we'd definitely win.

Let's tiptoe away now, before they spot us. Did you notice who's playing the piano for them? It's Dishy Dave. He's the one who started this whole thing off by saying we were good. I wonder what he thinks of the Hippo Girls? And why didn't we think of asking him to play the piano for us, instead of deciding to accompany ourselves? It just never crossed our minds, and it's too late now. The M&Ms really would accuse us of copying them then!

None of us could wait for Friday to come. We were still arguing about which song to do, but we'd more or less decided on Mama, because it was slow. That made it easier for us to sing and play. There was no way my fingers on the guitar could have kept up with the pace of Wannabe!

I was hoping - really desperately hoping - that Stuart would be going out till late, so we could use his room. That's what happened last time we had a sleepover at my place. His room is much bigger than mine, and he's got a TV and video in there, so we could have played my Spice Girls video.

When I asked him, though, he said he wasn't sure what he was doing that night.

"Meanie!" I told him.

"Who owes her big brother loads of money, eh?" he reminded me, with a yah-boo kind of expression on his spotty face. Then he held his hand up, saying, "Pay up and I might be able to afford to go out on Friday."

He knew Dad didn't give me my pocket money until Saturday, so there was no way that I could. I went to my room and had a quick sulk. Then I sorted out my sock drawer. I'd intended to do that for ages as I couldn't find any proper pairs any more and had gone to school that morning wearing one white sock and one cream one.

I'd spent all day expecting the M&Ms to notice and make fun of me, but they were far too busy boasting about how brilliant they were at being the Spice Girls, and how no other Spice Girls act stood a chance against them. They didn't know I'd seen their dancing hippos routine. They were so sad.

It got to Friday and we still didn't know if Stu was going out or not.

Tom, my next oldest brother, wasn't. He had made up his mind to enter a picture in an art competition in one of his weird magazines.

For a whole week, he'd spent every night in his room, drawing and painting. Every morning, he'd stagger down with his full waste-paper bin, dropping screwed up sheets of paper all down the stairs. I swooped on one and when I un-crumpled it,

I saw it was an amazing science fiction type of picture, complete with space ships and aliens and weird creatures with horns and antennae and tentacles, all in brilliant orange and slime green.

"Hey! Give me that back!" he shouted, and went all red with embarrassment.

"It's good," I told him. "Can I keep it?"

He looked pleased. "All right," he agreed.

I un-crumpled another one. It was seriously loony, with lots of funny purple creatures and bright red cactus plants.

"It was supposed to be Life On Mars, but it went wrong," he explained.

He snatched it out of my hand and tore it to shreds. Buster came bounding up the stairs and ate them.

"He'll be sick now. Red and purple sick, all over the carpet," Tom said, putting me right off my Coco Pops.

The first big disaster of our rehearsal was that Fliss hadn't brought the guitar.

"I looked in the shed but it wasn't there. Andy drove me here, anyway. I couldn't have brought it because he'd have seen it," she said.

At least Frankie had remembered her keyboard, so all was not lost. She reckoned it wouldn't take long to learn the tune from my tape. At least we'd still be able to practise.

Last time we'd held a sleepover at my house, we'd all been seriously into cucumber. We'd gone off it now. Celery was our new thing. It was so nice and crunchy and didn't give you the burps like cucumber did. So when Mum had asked me yesterday what kind of food we'd like, I'd told her to give us lots of celery.

Mum had made cheese and celery sandwiches, baked potatoes with pineapple and celery stuffing, and a big salad with loads of celery in.

There were two pizzas, one vegetarian, as both Frankie and I are veggie, and a ham and mushroom one for the others, plus all the usual crisps and cakes, and a huge bag of popcorn. Oh, and lots of lemonade and Coke.

"What's that?" Rosie asked, pointing to the plate in the middle of the kitchen table.

We all looked where Rosie was pointing. I'd thought it was a bit of Dad's wonky pottery which Mum had turned into a table decoration, but on close inspection, which involved prodding it a bit, it turned out to be a pile of celery sticks, arranged as a kind of mountain with the curly leaves looking like bushes on top, and tiny flakes of carrot stuck on like flowers.

"Weird!" said Frankie. "Really weird."

I had to agree with her. It was very weird indeed.

We weren't sure whether it was intended to be eaten, or just looked at, but Fudge solved it for us by leaping on the table, which she wasn't supposed to do, striding between our plates and knocking the celery heap over with her tail. After that, none of us wanted to eat it at all, as it was covered in cat hairs.

I'd told everyone to bring some Spice Girls costumes with them, so after we'd eaten the proper food, we took the crisps and things up to my room and got down to sorting out our clothes.

The bathroom's next to my bedroom. It soon got turned into an extra changing room, as it's got a big mirror in it. Fliss and Rosie were in there when suddenly we heard an ear-splitting scream!

Had they found a humongous spider in there, or was it something worse...?

CHAPTER SEVEN

Before any of us could arm ourselves with spider-killing weapons, there was a screech of, "Get out! Go away!" and the bathroom door slammed so hard that the pictures on my bedroom wall rattled.

Well, anyone knows that spiders can't understand English. So whatever was in the bathroom had to have more intelligence than a spider. Buster? One of the cats?

When we dashed out to see what the matter was, we found my brother Tom standing there. Now, the average spider has considerably more brains than Tom. I mean, surely he could hear bumps and voices and know that the bathroom was occupied?

Of course, there isn't a lock on the door. It broke ages ago and Dad never got round to fitting a new one, though bathroom door locks are about the most important thing in a house. I mean, you don't want someone walking in when you're on the toilet, do you?

Tom was standing there like a twit, with a clean T-shirt and a pair of underpants in his hand.

"I was only going to have a bath," he complained.

"A bath? You had one last month! Don't you think it's a bit soon for another one?" I said.

"Perhaps he's got a girlfriend," Frankie said.

To my amazement, Tom went bright red.

"He has! He has! Tom's got a girlfriend, Tom's got a girlfriend," sang Frankie.

"No, I haven't!" he said.

He bolted back into his bedroom and banged his door shut, making my pictures rattle again. I plonked myself down so hard on my bed that I bounced.

"I can't believe it!" I exclaimed. "Tom? He can't have a girlfriend. He's never been interested in girls."

"He's nearly fifteen. He could be," said Kenny.

"I think he's quite hunky," said Fliss, wiggling back into my room in her silver dress and matching shoes. She thinks anything male is hunky. She probably even fancies Buster!

"Better looking than Ryan Scott?" asked Frankie.

Fliss refused to answer.

"I'm going to write Fliss Loves Tom and put it under his door," said Frankie, looking round for some paper.

"Don't you dare!" screamed Fliss, flying at her and grinding a paper plate of crisps to dust on the carpet.

"No, don't. He'll get upset. He's really shy," I told her.

I thought it was really funny, though. He'd be in for a good teasing from me tomorrow.

I tried the red wig on. Once they'd stopped laughing, the others thought I looked quite like Ginger Spice. She likes shiny clothes and I'd made a black plastic mini skirt out of a piece of bin-liner.

I wore a black T-shirt with Stu's old black leather jacket over it, and my winter boots. I was sure Stu wouldn't mind my borrowing his jacket. He hadn't worn it for ages as it had got a bit small for him. I was boiling hot, but I tried not to moan. I knew the Spice Girls wouldn't have complained. Some of their video was shot in the boiling hot desert, yet they still jumped around and danced. They're amazing. Really professional. So we had to be the same.

Frankie looked great in a leopard print T-shirt of her mother's, worn as a dress. Rosie had a black bikini top on and a black skirt which was really a stretchy jersey top of Mum's.

Kenny just had her normal clothes on, Leicester City T-shirt and track suit bottoms. She really did look like Sporty Spice.

Frankie balanced the keyboard on the windowsill. She knocked over one of my china horses, but luckily it didn't break or I'd have broken her!

I hit the power button and fast-forwarded the tape player to Mama. The second Frankie's finger hit a key, I knew we were in deepest, darkest Doom-with-a-capital-D. Instead of sounding like a keyboard, it made a buzzing sound, as if twenty thousand bluebottles were trapped in it.

"You haven't just spilt your lemonade on that, have you?" I asked her.

"No." She frowned. Then she said, "I did upset a strawberry yogurt over it yesterday..."

"You're hopeless, Frankie!" Kenny told her.

Frankie tried every note, but they all sounded the same. She had really truly wrecked it. Now what were we going to do?

"We might as well give up," said Kenny.

She cracked the tab on a can of Coke, took a swig and passed it around. We all had some. Coke often gives me the hiccups, because it's fizzy. But not this time. Even my hiccups were too depressed to hic. They stayed in my middle, in hiding.

"I want to go to the loo," said Rosie.

"Tom's in the bath," Fliss reminded her.

"I can't wait. I'm desperate!" Rosie wailed.

"There's another loo downstairs," I reminded her. "Through the kitchen and turn right."

It was the original outside loo that had been built for our old-fashioned house. You had to be tough in those days. If you wanted to go to the loo in winter, you had to grab your wellies and brolly and risk sprouting icicles between leaving the kitchen door and entering the bog.

Good old Dad had put a nice little plastic

conservatory roof over it, which meant you couldn't get wet any more. Mum hated it because horrid, slimy moss grew on it - the roof, not the loo - and she had to climb on a chair to scrub it off with a brush.

"Come with me, someone, in case I get lost," Rosie said.

"I'll come. I want to go, too," said Frankie.

Off they went, and while they were gone, Kenny, Fliss and I leafed through *Girl Power*, our Spice Girls book, to see if anything about our costumes needed changing.

By now, I'd got so hot that I'd taken Stu's leather jacket off. I slung it on the bed but it fell on the floor and guess what? It went right to the spot where the cake had got squashed. Isn't that typical? I told you what I thought about us being grot magnets! I'd just have to wipe it down before I sneaked it back on the coat hook in the hall.

"You know what?" I said to Fliss. "I reckon I could make myself a top out of the spare bits of bin-liner. I kicked them under my bed."

I knelt down to look at them. My knees got all wet from the spilt lemonade. I pulled the bits of bin-bag out. Then I remembered the scissors were in the bathroom.

And so was Tom! Now we could get our

own back on him.

I beckoned to the others and we lined up by the bathroom door, trying not to giggle.

"One, two, three," I whispered. Then I yelled, "Charge!" and we burst the door open and galloped in.

Rats! He'd gone. Only a scummy line round the bath and a steamed-up mirror told us he'd ever been in there at all.

I got the scissors, laid the bin-liner on the floor and started to cut.

"That's funny," I said. "It's only plastic. It should be easier to cut than this."

Kenny had gone a funny shade. Sort of pale, with her eyes all bulgy as if she'd seen something nasty. "Er, Lyndz..." she said.

"What?" I frowned at her, wondering why she was looking at me like that. Had someone - The Goblin, perhaps - just turned me into a toad without me knowing anything about it?

I snatched up the piece of black plastic I'd been cutting. I realised what had gone wrong when my stripy cotton rug came up with it. I'd managed to cut through that as well.

"Mum's going to murder me!" I said, my face going as pale with horror as Kenny's.

"If you put some things on it, maybe she

won't notice," Fliss said.

There normally were loads of things on my carpet, like books and shoes. Fliss was right. I started to breathe normally again.

There was a knock on my door. "Reggie-Veggie!" said Frankie's voice. It was our password for the night. We always had one, for every sleepover, to keep out people we didn't want to come in.

"Enter, Friend!" I said.

Frankie and Rosie were looking really pleased with themselves.

"I think I've solved all our problems!" Frankie said.

CHAPTER EIGHT

I don't know about you, but when someone says they've solved all my problems, I expect them to have come up with something really good. Instead, Frankie and Rosie stood in the doorway arguing.

"It was me who heard it first!" Rosie said, looking indignantly at Frankie.

"Heard what?" I asked, shooting Fliss and Kenny a look which said quite plainly that these two had left their brains behind in the outside bog.

"We were passing the door of the babies' room when we heard it," Rosie went on.

She meant the room where my two little brothers, four-year-old Ben and baby Spike, sleep. It's on a kind of half landing, between the ground floor and the floor where my bedroom is.

"It was in tune with the album. We could still hear the song as we went downstairs. Couldn't we, Rosie?" Frankie said.

"I haven't a clue what you mean," I said.

"A musical instrument. As in bong-plink," said Frankie, giving me a pitying look.

Bong-plink? I couldn't think of anything that went bong-plink, unless it was her keyboard being thrown out of the window.

We all went down to listen, but we couldn't hear a thing. The babies slept with their door ajar. I went in. Ben had fallen asleep with his xylophone on the bed next to him and the stick to bong it with still in his hand.

I gently slipped it out of his fingers while Frankie picked up the xylophone. We all tiptoed away.

Back in my room, Frankie hit a few bongs and plinks and began to sing - or rather, groan - Mama.

"We can't use this!" I cried. "It's a baby's instrument. Everyone would laugh. The M&Ms would wet themselves!"

Everyone except Frankie agreed with me. She continued to play it. We all joined in singing. Suddenly, I saw the funny side and started laughing. That set everyone else off, until we were rolling about on the bed and on the floor, kicking our legs in the air and shrieking helplessly.

Next moment, there was a thunderous knocking on my door. We all held our breath, trying to stop laughing. It was Mum. She came in, looking very cross. Some extremely loud wailing was coming from somewhere behind her.

"What's this about you taking Ben's xylophone off him?" she said. "He came downstairs to find me, crying his eyes out."

Her eyes swept the room, till they reached Frankie, who was trying to hide it under a cushion.

Mum swooped on it. "Here you are, darling," she said.

My little brother appeared in the doorway and snatched the instrument to his chest. His big, wet eyes looked accusingly at me.

"But he was asleep when I took it!" I said.

"Wasn't asleep!" said Ben.

"Come back to bed, darling," Mum said, taking his hot, sticky hand. "And as for you, it's time you got those clothes off and started thinking about bed yourselves. You're making far too much noise. Spike's awake now, as well."

"But it's much too early to go to bed," I grumbled.

Trust Rosie to give a great big yawn!

"See? Someone's tired," Mum said. "Now, I want to see this bedroom light off, next time I come upstairs."

"Yes, Mum," I said.

It wasn't like my easy-going mother to get cross, but I'd heard her having a row with Dad earlier. She'd asked him the fatal question, when was our house ever going to get finished? She said she was sick of tripping over ladders and paintpots and never knowing where a door or window was going to appear next. I didn't hear any answer, I guess Dad had just shrugged and looked vague as usual.

We felt quite depressed, what with the ticking-off from Mum, and not being able to rehearse. So we all got washed and into our jim-jams, and then into our sleeping bags.

Usually, when there's a sleepover at my place my bed is taken right out and we all line up on the carpet. But tonight Dad had forgotten.

I decided there was enough room for two in my bed, one at either end. We did a dip-dip-dip to decide who it should be.

Just my luck to be landed with Lanky

Frankie, the tallest of us all. It was her big, smelly feet I was going to have to put up with next to my face all night.

Before we even tried to get off to sleep, we sang our club song, which we had to do all the hand movements to.

"Down by the river there's a hanky-pankyyy,
With a bull-frog sitting near the hanky-pankyyy.
With an ooh-ah, ooh-ah, hey, Mrs Zippy, with a 1-2-3 OUT!"

We sing the song sitting up, and on the word OUT! we all lie down as fast as we can. The first one to lie down turns off her torch, then everyone else turns theirs off until everyone's torch is out.

Then we start the serious business of trying to go to sleep, which involves Rosie twizzling around this way and that, until she finally curls up in a ball with her thumb in her mouth, while Kenny makes noises like a dog with a cold, snuffling and grumping.

Luckily for me, Frankie falls asleep in one position and stays that way all night. Sometimes Fliss has a nightmare. She'll sit bolt upright and scream, terrifying the rest of us.

Tonight, though, nobody made a sound. It was as if they were all dead. Then, through the darkness, came a whisper.

"Is anybody asleep?"

There was a chorus of whispers back. "No," we all said.

I flicked on the bedside lamp. Then I heard Mum coming back up the stairs, so I switched it off again and we all lay dead still, except that the bed was shaking as Frankie was trying not to giggle.

We heard Mum flush the loo. Then she went back downstairs. I switched the lamp on again and we all sighed with relief.

"Anyone got any food left?" Kenny asked. "I'm starving."

"So are we," said Fliss and Rosie.

"And me," Frankie joined in.

I found some cheese and onion crisps and half a carton of orange juice, so we shared them out.

Then we tried to go to sleep again, but none of us could. Rosie started humming Mama and one by one, the others joined in. Oh, why did the M&Ms have Dave playing piano for them? I thought. It just wasn't fair! Here were we with no piano, not even

Frankie's keyboard. Not even a guitar.

Suddenly, I thought about Stuart's group. All the instruments were lying about upstairs in the attic, just begging to be played. Stu was out - yes, my rotten brother had gone out after all, and hadn't told me, so I could use his room.

Mum and Dad were down on the ground floor. They'd never hear. Tom would think it was Stu, come back with his friends, and he wouldn't dare interrupt them.

It was a shiny-bright, mega-brilliant opportunity. All I had to do was find the chords to Mama on the guitar and we'd be sure to win our class heat and be allowed to sing in the charity show.

My pillow felt lumpy. I felt beneath it and guess what? There was a big bag of squashed marshmallows stuffed under it. Someone must have hidden them earlier, intending to scoff them in secret later on. It wasn't me.

Did I hear you say, "For a change"? You did? That's really mean of you. I don't pig out all the time. Just most of it. I don't eat when I'm asleep.

"Hey, everyone," I said. "I've found some marshmallows." See? I'm a generous, caring, sharing person!

I switched my bedside light on again. Everyone was already sitting up, waiting for a marshmallow.

"In a minute," I said. "First of all we've got a quest."

We all love stories with quests in, where the knight has to ride round the kingdom until he's slayed the dragon, or saved the princess.

"Ooh!" said Rosie. "What is it?"

"To get up to the attic and shut ourselves in, without being heard. And then we're really going to rehearse!"

CHAPTER NINE

It wasn't easy getting five people up to the attic in total silence. There isn't even a real staircase, just a kind of ladder that Dad made, while he's thinking of where to position the proper stairs. We might get stairs in ten years' time, just as I might get my new attic bedroom by the time I've grown up and left home!

The floor of our loft is covered in hardboard and a motheaten old carpet covers a lot of it. At least it's got electric light. If we'd had to use torches, it would have been dead spooky.

I pressed the switch and a bare lightbulb lit up. It dangled from a cord draped over one of the rafters. There wasn't any furniture up there, apart from two old plastic chairs which used to live in the garden.

There were probably loads of spiders lurking in corners. It didn't pay to look too closely.

I carefully closed the hatchway.

"Look at that!" I said.

"Wow!" exclaimed Rosie.

All the instruments a band could ever need were lying there where Stu and his mates had left them. Stu's saxophone was on the floor, propped against the bass drum. The guitar was leaning against the side of the water tank.

There was a bass guitar, too, which Frankie picked up.

"This is easy, it's only got four strings," she said, and twanged them. "How do you plug it in?" she asked.

I didn't know. But what I did know was how to plug in the tape player which Stu had left up there. It was a far more complicated one than mine and it had two cassettes in it.

I took one out. It had no label on it saying what it was, so I chucked it on the floor and put the Spice Girls tape on. The music sounded great, up in the echoey attic.

"There aren't any bats up here, are there?" asked Fliss, glancing nervously at the rafters.

"We found a dead pigeon when we first moved in," I told her, and watched her shudder.

"How about ghosts?" asked Fliss. She's genuinely scared of them, and can't watch spooky films, not even Gremlins, or Ghostbusters.

Just then the wind blew and rustled some polythene Dad had used to cover a hole he'd cut in the roof. Fliss screamed. The rest of us laughed at her.

"I'm cold," Rosie complained.

"You won't be in a minute," I said.

It was draughty in the attic, and we were only wearing our pyjamas. But I switched the Spice Girls on and as soon as we started to dance, we warmed up.

Frankie picked up the bass guitar and danced around with it. She made great swoops of her hand and bashed the strings. She looked like a real rock star.

Kenny got behind the drums. There was a slight crunch as she accidentally trod on the tape I'd taken out of Stu's cassette machine.

"Oh dear," she said.

"Don't worry, it's a blank one," I told her. Kenny looked perfect as a drummer.

"Go, girl, go!" Fliss shouted, as she picked up some drumsticks and took a wild swipe at the cymbal.

She hit it so hard that it fell off its stand. Fliss laughed so much that she had to get down and roll on the floor. When she stood up again, she was covered in dust and started coughing like mad.

"Bash her on the back," Kenny said to me, as I was nearest.

So I hit her.

"Ow! That really hurt, Lyndz," she complained.

"Sorry, I was only trying to help," I said. Honestly, you go off people sometimes! Especially when they're coughing in your face and their breath smells of cheese and onion crisps.

"Hey, Lyndz! The music's stopped!" yelled Frankie. "Shall I turn the tape over?"

"No! Don't touch a thing. Let me do it," I said.

I couldn't risk letting anyone break Stu's tape player. I was already deep in deadly debt to him, to the tune of a couple of quid. Imagine if I owed him hundreds of pounds! I'd still be paying him back by the time I left school!

I turned the tape over and pressed the Start button. Soon, the words of Mama were floating out and we all joined in.

"Turn it up louder," begged Rosie.

I turned it up a bit more. Not too much. I didn't want my parents to know we were up here. We'd have got into real trouble.

But, now that the music was louder, we really got into it. We'd never sung so well in our lives.

"Mama I love you, Mama my friend..."

We sounded better than the Spice Girls. Much better. But then, they didn't have an echoey, spidery attic to sing in, only a recording studio.

"Let's put it on again," said Fliss, when the track came to an end.

"Okay," I said, even though Who Do You Think You Are had started, which was good to dance to and always made me think of Ryan Scott. ("Who do you think you are? Some kind of superstar?" That was Ryan Scott to a T!)

I'd spotted a guitar propped up in the corner. It wasn't an electric one, so I knew I could play it. As soon as the record started, I fumbled around, trying to find the chords. The guitar wasn't quite in tune with the song.

"Stop a minute!" I shouted.

Everybody groaned.

"I was just getting into that," Frankie complained.

"Hard luck. I've got to tune this guitar," I said.

Luckily, I knew how to do it because I'd watched Stu's friend. I twiddled the knobs and the pitch of the strings went up or down. Soon, it sounded reasonably okay.

I put Mama back on again and began experimenting with the four chords I knew. And, miracle of miracles, with a bit more fumbling, I could just about play it!

"I've got it!" I said. "We can do our Spice Girls act after all! Just so long as I can borrow this guitar."

If Stu's mate had said "No," I'd have taken it anyway. Anything to beat the pathetic M&Ms.

"We'd better run through the song one more time, without the record," Kenny said sensibly.

"Yes. I couldn't hear my singing above your horrible croak," Fliss said to Kenny.

Kenny poked her tongue out at Fliss. It looked as though a scrap might break out, so I quickly picked up the guitar.

This was the real test. And, do you know what? We sounded great. When Frankie started sounding like a sick crow, Kenny nudged her hard in the middle to shut her up a bit. Rosie, Fliss and myself were in tune, and Kenny was most of the time.

When we'd got to the end of the song, I put the guitar down on the floor and jumped up in the air.

"Oh, wow!" I said.

"Yeah, wow!" said Kenny.

"Brilliant!" said Rosie.

We all hugged each other and started hopping round in a circle. Big mistake. For that's when it happened. Kenny gave an blood-curdling screech - and started to disappear before our eyes!

CHAPTER TEN

"Kenny!" I shrieked, grabbing at her.

The others were all rushing round flapping like headless chickens.

"Frankie! Help me!" I yelled, as I hung on to Kenny for dear life.

Now that I was next to her, I could see what had happened. It was all Dad's fault, as usual. There was just one place in the whole attic where he hadn't put any hardboard, and Kenny's foot had found it and gone between the rafters and through the flimsy floor.

"She's not going to fall down to the next floor, is she?" Rosie asked anxiously.

"Don't move!" I ordered Kenny.

"Just as if I could! Isn't anyone going to

ask if I'm all right?" Kenny said. Although she's the toughest one of us, her voice sounded quite wobbly.

"Er... are you all right?" I asked her. I was still clutching her arm, trying to save her.

"I would be if you'd just let go. Your fingers are digging into me," she said.

"All right, all right. I was just trying to stop you falling forty thousand feet into the Pit of Hell!" I said.

I let go. She didn't seem to be falling any further.

"Can you get up, Kenny?" Fliss asked.

She was in a funny position with one leg spread out at an angle. She tried to heave herself up, but it was no good.

"My leg's completely stuck in the hole," she said. "It doesn't hurt, it's just stuck and I can't move it."

"Let's have a go at pulling her out," Frankie suggested.

"Yes, we'll treat it as a tug-o'war," said Fliss.

"Don't you dare! What do you think I am? A piece of rope?" said Kenny.

I took hold of one of her arms and Rosie grabbed the other. Frankie got her leg. Fliss stood there and counted.

"One... two... three... PULL!"

"OUCH!" screeched Kenny as we all heaved as hard as we could.

But Kenny didn't budge and we all lost our grip on her and fell over.

Frankie fell on top of Kenny, adding major squashing to her list of injuries.

Rosie grabbed hold of something to save herself. It was an amplifier which we'd used as a table for the food. The marshmallows fell right into the mouth of the saxophone, followed by Rosie's wildly waving arm. Her hand went right down inside it, wedging the marshmallows in there for ever.

As she tried to get up, she kicked the drumkit. Bits flew off and clattered all over the floor.

I cannoned into Fliss. She staggered backwards and - oh, no! There was a terrifying crunching sound.

"Wh-what have you done?" I asked her, my voice all shaky with terror. I knew from the noise that something had got broken. Something that spelled major T-R-O-U-B-L-E.

I was right.

"I've trodden on the guitar. Look at it!" Rosie said. She went pale and started to cry.

I felt like being sick. She'd trodden on the neck of the instrument and it had broken in two. It was absolutely ruined. How were we ever going to pay for a new one?

Rosie was down on her knees, examining the damage.

"How are we going to do our Spice Girls routine now? The M&Ms will win and nobody will hear me sing!" Fliss wailed.

I thought personally that the school might be very glad not to hear Fliss sing - but none of us wanted the gruesome M&Ms to triumph over us. Beaten by our worst enemies! It was a fate worse than death.

"Maybe I can borrow Andy's guitar," I said to Fliss, who'd joined Rosie on the floor to inspect the broken guitar.

"This is Andy's guitar," she said doomily. "Look..."

She pointed to a label inside it. Andy's name and telephone number were on it.

"He must have done that in case he lost it," she said.

I got cross then. "Fancy lending it to Stu's group. What a daft thing to do. He might have known something would happen to it," I said.

"Stop worrying about a stupid guitar. What about me?" said a lonely voice from the corner of the attic.

Poor old Kenny. We'd forgotten all about her!

"Maybe, if we make the hole a bit bigger, we could get her leg out," Frankie suggested.

"Okay, let's have a go," I said.

Just as we were about to start our Kenny Rescue Mission, we heard the one sound we didn't want to hear.

Voices on the landing below us. Boys' voices.

"Ssh!" I hissed warningly.

We all fell dead silent.

Then: "Hey! There's a leg sticking through my ceiling!"

The yell came from Tom's room. He must have just gone in there.

Pandemonium broke out on the floor below as Stu and his mates all rushed in to see. The next minute, they were all pounding up the stairs into the attic. Our doom was sealed.

"Quick!" I said to the others. "Try and get the drumkit back together. And hide the guitar!"

"I don't want boys to see me in my pyjamas!" wailed Fliss, hiding behind the amplifier. None of us did. It was seriously embarrassing. But there wasn't a thing any of us could do about it.

The hatchway door flew open with a bang and my oldest brother stuck his head through.

"I might have known!" he shouted. "Trust you and your friends to cause trouble, Lyndz. I hope making a hole in the ceiling is all you've done..."

We all looked at one another guiltily. The wrecked guitar was behind Rosie. She'd better not budge one inch, or all would be revealed! We had to get away from the scene of crime as quickly as possible.

"Stu, it wasn't Kenny's fault that she fell through the ceiling. Dad hadn't put any hardboard there," I said.

"Well, I knew that bit wasn't safe. Why didn't you look where you were going? I suppose we'd better get her out. Mick, Tony, give us a hand, will you?"

The boys broke off a few bits of floor and ceiling and soon had Kenny free.

There was another yell from Tom downstairs. "Hey! All those bits of ceiling went all over my best painting. It's ruined! The paint was still wet," he moaned. "How can I go in for the competition now?"

I felt doom strike again. I knew I'd never hear the end of it now. Tom would never forgive me.

At least Kenny was okay, though. Now we just had the broken guitar to deal with. Or so we thought…

"Before I go and tell Mum and Dad about all this, what were you doing up here in the first place?" Stu asked me.

"We were rehearsing for a charity show at school. All the best acts get entered in it. We're going to be the Spice Girls," I told him.

"Well, the Spice Girls had better get to bed because it's nearly ten o'clock and we're going to have an hour's band practice ourselves," Stu said.

Oh no! The drumkit would fall apart the moment Mick touched it. And what about Andy's guitar?

"What are you waiting for? We want to get started. Get going, you lot!" Stu said.

Rosie didn't dare move. Her face was panic-stricken. Her lips formed the words, "What am I going to do?"

Some delaying tactics were needed.

"Just let me get my Spice Girls tape," I said, moving towards the tape player.

My brother looked as if he'd just heard that the universe was going to end in five minutes' time. He went white.

"You haven't been playing your Spice Girls tape on that machine over there, have you?" he said faintly.

"Uh-huh," I said.

There was a moment's total silence. Then his face grew fiery red.

"You idiot! You twit! You total amoeba-brain. How could you? Do you know what you've done?" he thundered.

I shook my head.

"That's a very complex machine which we borrowed from another band. We had it specially set up to record our music on. You've wiped out our demo tape that we were going to send to a record company. It took us three weeks to record. I'll get you for this, Lyndz!"

He took a step towards me, meaning to pull my hair or something. I ducked, he staggered and - guess what? - his enormous great foot stamped right on to Andy's guitar. Ker-unch!

Whoopee! A huge weight lifted off me. Now it was Stuart's turn to look scared and guilty.

"Oh crikey," he said. "Look what I've gone and done."

"I told you to put it back in its case," Tony said. "But you said you couldn't find it."

Just then, Mum and Dad arrived on the scene and we were all in trouble - all except for Tom. Everyone was very sympathetic about his painting and Dad helped him clear all the rubble out of his bedroom.

Mum ticked us off good and proper. "You girls had no right to go up there. You should be asleep in bed!" she said.

Then she started fussing over Kenny, who had a few nasty bruises. Out came the Savlon and then she offered us a real treat - hot chocolate. Not just for Kenny, but for all of us, because we were all shivering with cold by now. Yum!

But, just as she was bringing in the tray, her toe caught in something and she tripped. Five mugs of steaming hot chocolate leapt off the tray like horses tackling a six foot fence. Up into the air they went, spraying chocolate all over my bedroom wall.

Our mouths fell open in horror, and stayed that way as the mugs descended in slow motion on to my white bedspread. A brown, sludgy oasis of chocolate formed a widening pool. I stared at it, horrified.

"Don't just stand there gawping like goldfish. Help me clear up, girls!" snapped Mum.

No mugs were broken. Mum thought it was her fault, and kept apologising as she took the wet bedding away and brought in the spare duvet.

It was the last of the hot chocolate, worse luck. She'd emptied the tin. Still apologising, Mum saw that we were all tucked up in our respective sleeping places.

She was just standing with her hand on the light switch, about to say goodnight and turn it out, when it suddenly occurred to her to ask a question: "I wonder what I caught my foot on? Whatever it is, it's dangerous and I'd better find it before there are any more accidents."

Well, I lay there feeling completely innocent. So much else had happened that evening that I had forgotten all about chopping up my rug with the scissors.

Mum found it, of course. And then came the real punishment. There were to be no more sleepovers in our house, ever again. Mind you, that's what she said last time, so I didn't really believe her. But you never know with Mums...

She confiscated my Spice Girls tape, too. And my video of them. That meant we didn't have the words to Mama, because they were written down on the inner sleeve of the cassette. So it was bye-bye competition, especially as we had no chance of borrowing a guitar from anyone.

I could just see the M&Ms and their witchy friends, smirking all over their fat faces when they discovered we'd dropped out and they were the only Spice Girls after all. Emma had got her revenge. Hate, hate, hate!

THE END

So that's it! We're all grounded again.

Stu says I owe him all my pocket money for ever and ever, for those crisps and things we ate the other day, and for ruining his band's demo tape. It's really unfair! How were we to know that we'd recorded the Spice Girls over one copy and that Kenny had trodden on the other? Fancy him not bothering to put a label on something as important as a demo tape.

Tom was beastly to me about his ruined painting, until I told him I thought the orange and slime green one he'd let me keep was even better. In the end he agreed with me, ironed out the creases and sent it off to the competition. I hope he wins, I really do.

In the meantime, Stu's given him his first real 'commission', which is when someone asks an artist to paint them something. He's asked Tom to paint a Spanish guitar. On cardboard, so it'll be stiff. It's going inside Andy's guitar case while his real guitar is being mended. It's just in case he comes round and asks if his guitar's okay. Stu will open the case and flash the piccy at him, then close it again quick!

Talking of Stu, he couldn't get a note out of his saxophone yesterday, so he's taken it into a repair shop - where, of course, they'll find loads of squishy marshmallows jammed down inside it. Uh-oh, more trouble!

Just in case you're thinking things are all doom and gloom, though, get this! Remember I told you we'd accidentally recorded the Spice Girls over Stu's demo tape? I managed to sneak up to the attic and grab it, which meant we could still rehearse. As we're currently banned from visiting each other, we stayed on late at school and persuaded Dishy Dave to play Mama for us on the piano, promising him a mega bar of his favourite choc.

A nasty throat bug has been sweeping school. We were praying that none of us would get it before the class heats. Luckily, we didn't. The heats were held in the school hall. Dave played the piano for us and I think we did Mama brilliantly. We'd changed into our Spice outfits, and the M&Ms hadn't thought of that. They were still in their ordinary school clothes.

When it came to the M&Ms' turn to perform Wannabe, we all looked at each other, scarcely breathing. This was it! We just had to be better than them, we had to! But they had Regina, whose voice is so much better than any of ours.

Dave played the introductory bars, Regina opened her mouth to sing - and no sound came out. Not a squeak. She'd caught the dreaded throat bug! Talk about laugh. We nearly had awful accidents, we laughed so hard. Luckily, we weren't the only ones laughing, or Mrs Weaver would have told us off.

They couldn't perform, so they were out of the contest. You should have seen their faces - especially when we ended up winning the class heat!

Now we go forward to the Grand Final in three weeks' time. Wish us luck! We've all decided it doesn't matter if we don't win, because we've done what we really wanted to do already. We've beaten the M&Ms and that's the best thing of all and something we'll gloat over for centuries.

Uh-oh, we'll have to scatter. I can hear Frankie charging down the path like a rhino in Doc Martens.

"Lyndz, Lyndz, where are you?" she's yelling. "You haven't seen my Nature exercise book, have you?"

I borrowed it so that I could copy her picture of a chaffinch. It was a very good drawing. She'd coloured it in with pastels. But pastels rub off, don't they? And I've just found out I've been sitting on the notebook all the time I've been talking to you. Look! There's no chaffinch left, just a nasty brown and pink smear. See that big bush over there? If I'm not around for dinner tonight, it means I'm still hiding behind it.

END

Order Form

To order direct from the publishers, just make a list of the titles you want and fill in the form below:

Name ....

Address ....

....

....

Send to: Dept 6, HarperCollins Publishers Ltd, Westerhill Road, Bishopbriggs, Glasgow G64 2QT.

Please enclose a cheque or postal order to the value of the cover price, plus:

UK & BFPO: Add £1.00 for the first book, and 25p per copy for each additional book ordered.

Overseas and Eire: Add £2.95 service charge. Books will be sent by surface mail but quotes for airmail despatch will be given on request.

A 24-hour telephone ordering service is available to holders of Visa, MasterCard, Amex or Switch cards on 0141- 772 2281.

Collins
An *Imprint of* HarperCollins*Publishers*